THE ADVENTURES OF RAINBOW FISH

INCLUDING:

 HarperCollins*Publishers*

The Adventures of Rainbow Fish:
Finders Keepers
The Dangerous Deep
Spike and the Substitute
Tattle Tale

RAINBOW FISH
FINDERS KEEPERS

Rainbow Fish was swimming
through the Coral Reef.
He was looking for colorful
shells for his collection.

What could that be? Rainbow Fish wondered.

He swam down for a closer look.

"It's so bright and shiny."

"Sea glass!" cried Rainbow Fish.

"It's so beautiful."

Rainbow Fish loved the sea glass.

He always carried it around—

pretty sea glass, with a hole in it.

One day after school,

Rainbow Fish couldn't find his sea glass.

"Oh, no! How could I have lost it?" he cried.

He searched every inch of the Coral Reef.

He looked everywhere but could not find it.

It wasn't at the Sunken Ship

or swirling in the Whirlpool.

It wasn't along Mrs. Crabbitz's shortcut.

Rainbow Fish was heartbroken.

His beautiful sea glass was gone.

A few days later, Little Blue jetted

through the Sunken Ship.

"Check out my lucky charm," he boasted.

"Hey, that's my sea glass!"

cried Rainbow Fish.

"I've been looking all over for it.

Where did you find it?"

"It's not your sea glass," said Little Blue.

"Yes it is. I found it and then I lost it,"

said Rainbow Fish.

"I've had this forever," said Little Blue.

"Oh, come on Little Blue," said Rosie.

"I saw you pick that up at the Oyster Beds

on the way to school."

"I must have dropped it at the
Oyster Beds when I went looking
for pearls with Puffer," said
Rainbow Fish.

"That doesn't prove anything!
Just because you lost a piece of sea glass
doesn't mean that this one is yours,"
cried Little Blue.

"Besides," said Little Blue,

"I've never seen you

with a piece of sea glass."

"I have an idea," said Dyna

as she took the piece of sea glass

and hid it behind her.

"Describe the sea glass to me,"
said Dyna.

"Little Blue, you start."

Little Blue hesitated.

"Well . . . it's um orange . . ." he said.

"You mean red," Rainbow Fish corrected.

"Right. That's what I meant. Red!"
Little Blue said.

"And it's . . . smooth and round,"
Little Blue added.

"You mean except for the hole,"
Rainbow Fish corrected.

"Of course. Except for the hole,"

said Little Blue.

"I got mixed up when you interrupted me."

"That's not what it sounds like to me,"
said Dyna.

Everyone agreed that the sea glass
belonged to Rainbow Fish.

"I found it, fair and square!"

shouted Little Blue.

"Finders keepers, losers weepers!"

"What if you lost something

you really loved?" asked Dyna.

"But it's not fair," cried Little Blue.

"Maybe Rainbow Fish could help
you find another piece of sea
glass," suggested Tug.

"We'll never find a piece of sea glass
like this one," said Little Blue.

"We can find one that's just as pretty,"
said Rainbow Fish.

"You can hold this one while we look."

Little Blue found a piece of sea glass.

It was bright yellow and very pretty.

Rainbow Fish had his own sea glass back.

They were both very happy.

WHAT WILL RAINBOW FISH
AND HIS FRIENDS
EXPLORE NEXT?

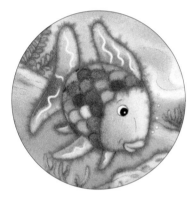

RAINBOW FISH
THE DANGEROUS DEEP

Text by Leslie Goldman

Illustrations by Benrei Huang

One morning, Miss Cuttle called
her school of fish to order.
"Old Nemo will be here soon
to tell us all about his days
as a famous explorer," she said.

"Hooray!" Rainbow Fish cheered.

"Old Nemo tells great stories."

"The one about the giant jellyfish

is the best," said Spike.

"It is one of my favorites, too,"

added Old Nemo.

He told stories all morning.

After Old Nemo left,

Miss Cuttle had a hard time

getting her class back to work.

They did not want to sort shells.

They wanted to fight off giant jellyfish

and find secret caverns.

Miss Cuttle could see that
her class needed a break.
"I think you are all still off
in one of Old Nemo's stories.
Let's take an early recess."

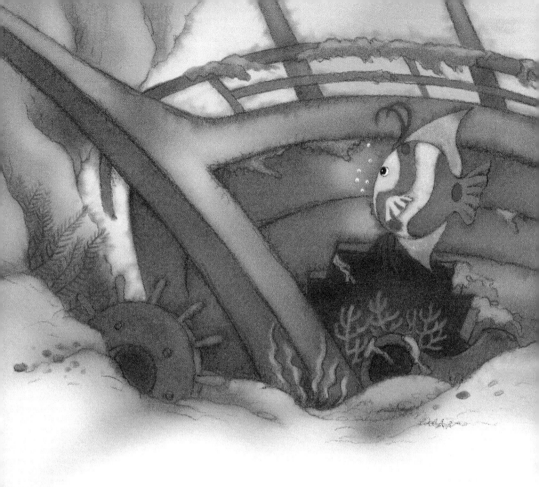

After Old Nemo's tales of the sea,
recess at the Sunken Ship was not
very exciting.

"We can pretend we are brave
explorers," said Angel.

"I have a better idea," said Spike.

"Let's explore the reef."

"That is a great idea," agreed
Rainbow Fish.
"But what will Miss Cuttle say?"
asked Angel.

"We will be back before she
even knows that we are gone,"
said Spike.

"Come on, follow me!"

Rainbow Fish, Spike, and Angel
jetted off toward the Oyster Beds.
"We can find a pearl just like Puffer did,"
Rainbow Fish said.

"It is not a real adventure
if someone has already done it,"
said Spike.

"What about the Crystal Caverns?"

asked Rainbow Fish.

"Ooh, they are so sparkly," added Angel.

"We have been there, too," said Spike.

"Old Nemo found them long ago."

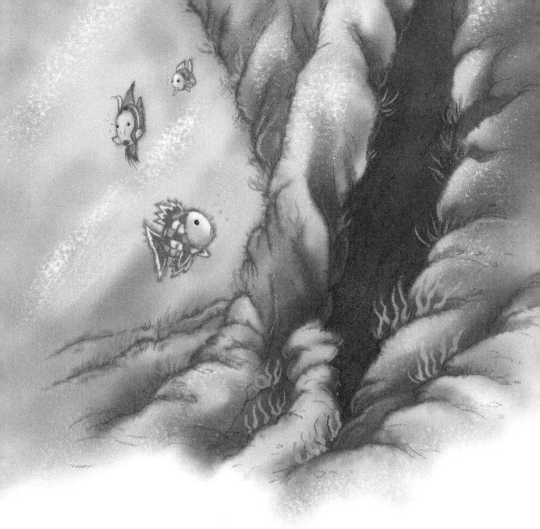

"Do you have any better ideas?"

asked Rainbow Fish.

"We can go to the volcano," said Spike.

"No one *ever* goes there."

Off they went.

Spike stopped at the edge

of the volcano.

"I dare you to take a closer look."

"But we are not allowed to,"

said Rainbow Fish.

"Don't be such a scaredy-catfish,"

said Spike.

Suddenly a dark shadow appeared.
As it moved closer, it grew bigger.
The fish were frozen with fear.
"We should have stayed at school,"
whispered Angel.

A loud voice boomed from the

shadow.

"Does Miss Cuttle know where

you are?"

It was Old Nemo.

"I am so glad it is you, Old Nemo,"

said Rainbow Fish.

"We were really scared."

"There is much to be afraid of
in the deep," said Old Nemo.
"You young fish are very lucky.
The ocean deep is no place
for you."

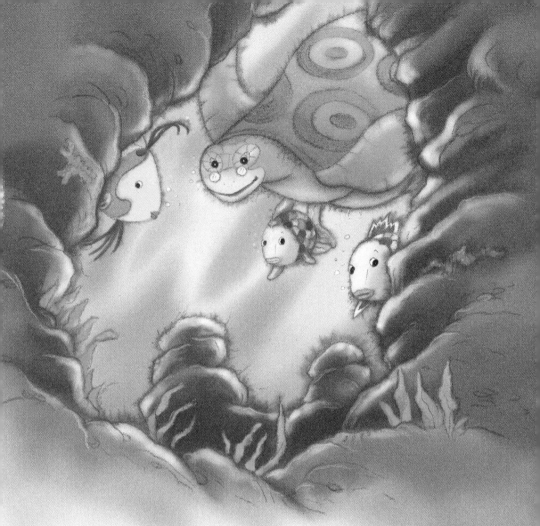

"We want to be brave
explorers," they said all at once.
"Many young fish dream about
the adventures that await them
in the deep," said Old Nemo.

"School is adventure enough
for young fish," said Old Nemo.

"You still have much to learn before you will be ready to explore the great beyond."

And with that, Old Nemo led them back to Miss Cuttle's school.

Rainbow Fish, Spike, and Angel
told Miss Cuttle they were sorry
for swimming off by themselves.
They promised never to do it again.
"I am just glad you are back safe
and sound," she replied.

Old Nemo was right.

School was the only adventure
they needed.

WHAT HAPPENS
WHEN SPIKE
MISBEHAVES IN CLASS?

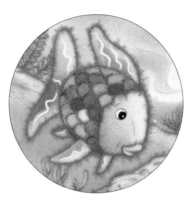

RAINBOW FISH
SPIKE AND THE SUBSTITUTE

Text by Leslie Goldman

Illustrations by Benrei Huang

Spike and Rainbow Fish
raced to school.
Today was the best day
of the week.
It was show-and-tell day.

All the fish in Miss Cuttle's class
loved show-and-tell.

It was a chance to share their
treasures with their friends.

Spike could not wait.

He had found something

extra-special to show his friends.

It was a piece of coral

shaped like a fish.

"Attention!" Miss Cuttle called.

"It is time to settle down

and start our day."

Everyone did.

Spike did his best to listen.

But all he could think about

was his great piece of coral.

He just could not wait

to show it off.

Quietly, Spike picked up

his piece of coral

and showed it to Rainbow Fish.

Soon, the two little fish forgot

all about Miss Cuttle's lesson.

"Spike," said Miss Cuttle,

"please put that away.

We have work to do."

Spike quickly put the coral away.

Paying attention was not easy.

Spike could not resist

taking out the coral again.

"Spike, you will have to wait for

show-and-tell like everyone else,"

Miss Cuttle said.

"You better be careful,"
said Rainbow Fish.
"Miss Cuttle only gives three
chances. You do not want
your coral to end up in the
treasure chest."

Spike knew this was true.

But, just before recess,

Spike thought to himself,

Miss Cuttle will not mind if I

take a quick look at my coral.

But Miss Cuttle did mind.

"Spike, you know the rules.

This is the third time that I have

asked you to put that away.

Now your treasure goes

in the treasure chest."

The rest of the day passed

very slowly for Spike.

He listened to the other students

talk about their treasures.

Spike wanted his coral back.

He was not sad. He was mad.

Later, Spike told Rainbow Fish,

"Miss Cuttle is mean.

That was not fair.

I wish she was not our teacher."

"Be careful what you wish for,"

warned Rainbow Fish.

The next morning Spike found

Mrs. Crabbitz in their cave classroom.

All the fish began to talk at once.

"Why is Mrs. Crabbitz here?"
asked Rosie.
"Where is Miss Cuttle?"
Rainbow Fish asked.

Mrs. Crabbitz cleared her throat.

"Settle down! Settle down!

Miss Cuttle is out sick.

I will be your teacher today.

I expect you all to behave,"

she said.

Everyone was sad that

Miss Cuttle was sick.

Everyone but Spike.

Mrs. Crabbitz quickly got the class
settled down and ready for work.
But she wasn't like Miss Cuttle.
Mrs. Crabbitz was very strict.

Mrs. Crabbitz yelled all day long.

School was not much fun

without Miss Cuttle.

The class missed their teacher.

Spike began to miss his teacher, too.

He wondered if Miss Cuttle

had stayed home because

he had misbehaved.

The more Spike thought about it,

the worse he felt.

When the class lined up for recess,

Spike was so upset that he swam

into a corner by himself.

"I am *not* going," he said.

"You cannot make me!"

"If you want to be alone,
that is fine. But you still
have to come outside,"
said Mrs. Crabbitz.

Spike knew he had to listen to
Mrs. Crabbitz, so he followed her
out to the Shipwreck.

"You can build a
sculpture while you are
all by yourself over here,"
said Mrs. Crabbitz as she gathered
rocks, shells, and seaweed.

"When I need time to think,

I build sculptures,"

said Mrs. Crabbitz.

Her pile quickly turned

into a beautiful sculpture.

Spike decided to make his own.

The rest of the day

passed quickly for Spike.

At the end of the lessons,

Spike stayed behind.

He told Mrs. Crabbitz

he was sorry for misbehaving.

The next morning,

Spike was happy to see

Miss Cuttle back at school.

Only one thing worried him:

Did Mrs. Crabbitz tell

her that he had misbehaved?

Miss Cuttle swam over to Spike
and said, "Mrs. Crabbitz told
me about your sculpture!
Would you like to share it at
show-and-tell?"

"You bet!" said Spike.

"I knew you would miss Miss
Cuttle," Rainbow Fish said.

WILL RAINBOW FISH
BE ABLE TO SAVE
A FRIENDSHIP?

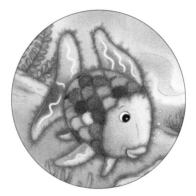

RAINBOW FISH
TATTLE TALE

Text by Sonia Sander

Illustrations by Benrei Huang

Rosie and Dyna were happy.

They were going to work together

on a science project.

"We will have the best project

in class," said Dyna.

"I know lots about growing algae."

Everything went well.

But Rosie and Dyna didn't always agree
on how to work together.

"Knock, knock," joked Rosie.

"Who is there?" asked Dyna.

"Sea," answered Rosie.

"Sea who?" asked Dyna.

"See that—we are almost done,"

said Rosie.

Dyna didn't think that was funny.

"We are *not* almost done.

We have not finished all of the

steps yet," said Dyna.

"We don't have to follow all of the directions," said Rosie.

"I want to do it right," said Dyna.

Just then Miss Cuttle called,

"Recess time!"

At the Shipwreck playground

all the fish talked about their

science projects.

"How is your algae project going?"
Rainbow Fish asked Dyna.
"We would be finished if Rosie did not
joke around so much," said Dyna.
Angel thought this was interesting news.

After recess Rosie played with their algae.

"Roses are red, violets are blue.

This brown algae is sticky like glue,"

sang Rosie.

Dyna was unhappy.

The algae was now brown.

It should have been green!

"Now we have to start over!"

After school Angel asked Rosie
how she liked working with Dyna.

"The project would be more fun if she didn't worry so much," said Rosie. "She always tells me to be more careful."

"Oh, dear," said Angel.

"It does not sound like their project

is going well at all."

Angel swam over to Rusty and said,

"I heard that Dyna is being bossy and

Rosie is acting like a clown!"

Rusty swam over to Spike and said,

"Rosie and Dyna aren't getting along."

"Rosie is a good partner," said Spike.

"I always have fun working with her."

116

"It's fun until Miss Cuttle asks to
see your work," said Rusty.
"You get in trouble if it's not
done."

Rusty liked working with Dyna.

"I would work with Dyna any time,"

said Rusty. "She's so careful."

118

"You mean *boring*," said Spike.
"Dyna wants to do all the work
herself."

Dyna and Rosie had heard every word.

Their feelings were hurt.

"I thought you were my friend," said Dyna.

"How could you say that I am bossy?"

Rosie said, "I didn't say you were

bossy. Honest!"

"I thought working with you would
be fun," said Rosie.
"But if you think I'm a clown I don't
want to work with you at all."

"That is not what I said," Dyna replied.

"Ask Rainbow Fish. He was there!"

Rainbow Fish hated to see his

friends upset.

He thought he knew how this

problem started.

"The story got mixed up as it was

repeated," he said.

"You two could still be partners,"

said Rainbow Fish.

"Rosie, you always have fun ideas.

Dyna, you can make anything work.

I bet if you tried again, you could

have the best science project."

So Rosie and Dyna made up

and tried to work together.

Rosie told Dyna all about her ideas.

Dyna told Rosie what algae needs to grow.
Together they figured out how
to complete their science project.

This time the algae did grow.

It grew into a beautiful castle.

Their project was a success.